CAUGHT LOOKING BY THE DROPOUT

Straight to Gay First Time Story

Michael Levi

ISBN: 9798421881230
Imprint: Independently published

1st edition

Cover design by: Michael Levi

CONTENTS

Title Page

Copyright

Chapter 1   1

Chapter 2   6

Chapter 3   11

Chapter 4   16

Chapter 5   21

Chapter 6   24

Sneak Peek: Caught Looking by the Quarterback   29

Bicurious Series and More   33

About the Author   35

CHAPTER 1

"Yeah, I'm just gonna get something," I said to my friend behind me, opening the door and halting when my eyes stumbled on something eye-destructive.

This was my room, so why the hell was Blake in here? He was half-naked, with his shirt off and holding, in his hands, one of my shirts. Was he desperate and looking for a shirt in my room? I couldn't tell, but I could tell this one thing – he worked out often.

Damn. I wasn't gay, but even someone like me had to admit it – his torso was perfect. One could run his hands over his lines, feel them for what they were, and they would walk out of that feeling that he was like a statue. Even from afar his muscles looked so taut, as though he was tense all the time.

I couldn't help but gulp, realizing that I thought that way of someone I'd first met not too long ago. When I got into college, a chain of events fucked up his academic career. Now…. Now he was just a dropout, and he shouldn't be in my room, even though part of me was enjoying what I was witnessing.

He used to be a swimmer. His body wasn't big, his muscles weren't too thick, and he didn't look heavy, either. He was just… perfect.

Now that I was thinking about it, what gym did he go to? I couldn't help but wonder, the thought that I'd stumble on him pumping iron making my skin warmer.

Dammit. What the hell was this thing sprouting up in me all

of a sudden? I shouldn't be having these feelings for another man, and I wasn't going to let them grow. That much was certain.

I cleared my throat again, catching the dropout's attention as he slowly turned his head. He was looking at me now, regarding me with compassion, toughness, and something else I couldn't put my finger on. I had my suspicion, but me being me, I didn't want to think that it meant anything relevant.

"Tom, it's so nice to see you. I didn't think that I was going to. I'm sorry." He shook his head dismissively. "I didn't intend to sneak into your room. I was just looking for a shirt and something for the cold. It's freezing outside, man."

I checked him out slowly, taking in the sight of this man in front of me. I couldn't help but feel that I was slacking off. I should work out harder at the gym, and perhaps, one day, even ask Blake for his schedule. I was pretty sure that he'd tell me what it was.

He held out his hand and I wrapped mine on it. Or maybe I should be saying that he engulfed my hand with his, showing his dominance. For a moment, I couldn't pull my hand back. His hand was firm, calloused, warm, and it was showing me he was the Alpha male in here.

It only made sense. Blake was slightly taller, bigger, heavier, and already had a perfect beard on his face. As for me? I couldn't even begin growing one. I had some hairs, but they held little potential. They weren't going to grow and cover my face, making it look older and more masculine like his.

The dropout opened his hand, letting go of mine. I didn't notice it at the time, but the way he was gripping my hand... I couldn't even breathe while he did that. It was like he was suffocating me, which was something that didn't happen often with me. And my dick grew larger in my pants, too. Noticing that, I blushed, though only slightly. I didn't want the dominating dropout noticing that.

I stepped to the drawer, opening it and grabbing a shirt. "Well, what do you think of this one? It's old, but I think that it probably fits you."

He grabbed the shirt, checking it out. He gave me a nod as he put it on slowly. As he did that, I couldn't help but feel a little sad that I couldn't see his exposed torso anymore. His skin was perfect, smooth, and very shiny, even under the dim light coming from the sun through the clouds.

I didn't know what was going on with me, but this morning I was feeling very willing to help anyone. It wasn't something that happened often with me. Growing up in a very poor environment, I learned how to put myself above others.

But I wanted to help this dropout as much as I could. It was like I was feeling a connection to him I thought I could never have. Not feeling worried about it, I knew it was going to pass and that I was going to return to my normal self pretty soon.

We were in front of the wardrobe. I stepped to the side, opening one of the side doors. My hands rummaged inside it as I looked for a jacket. Seconds later, I found an old one which should also fit him. I had it when I was younger and a little bigger than now.

I held it in front of me with both of my hands, checking out its exterior to make sure that it didn't have too many holes and tears in it. Satisfied with what I was looking at, I nodded and handed him the jacket.

Blake took it from my hands, put it on, making me feel a lot better than when I walked into the room. Knowing that his perfect chest wasn't something that my eyes could feast on, I felt like I could return to being my normal self.

I even puffed out my chest, which was something I didn't do often. It had nothing to do with my sense of insecurity or anything like that, I promised to myself.

And I didn't know why, but I could smell his perfume. I didn't even know that he was the kind of guy who wore perfume in the winter. But he did and the fragrance was very strong, intense, and intoxicating. I didn't know why I didn't notice it when I stepped into the room.

As he looked at me with kind eyes – the kind that shouldn't

really mean anything to me, but still did – he said, "Bro, there's this party going on that I need to go to right now. Wanna come with me? I'm not really allowed to bring guests, but I'm making an exception for you."

"A party? Where?" I asked, not really knowing if I should take him up on his offer. After all, I told my girlfriend that I was going to meet up with her in that Brazilian barbecue restaurant she liked so much. I didn't want to disappoint her, but Blake was also one of my best friends when he was still in college.

"At a friend's. Interested? I can take you there in my car."

Driving with Blake to a party? Call me crazy, but I never thought that this day would ever come. Nothing weird or wrong with it, just the fact that Blake never went anywhere with anyone that wasn't his girlfriend. And now, thinking about that, where was she even? I didn't know, but the look in his eyes was telling me that the party, for him, meant a lot more than what met the eyes…

I didn't want to think much of it and I didn't. I nodded and responded, "Sure, I think that going there would be pretty nice."

"Then, let's go," he said, waving his hand over his shoulder and making me follow him. As we crossed the living room on the first floor, I heard one of my roommates calling out to me, but I didn't respond. Strange. I never did that before. It was as though I was hanging out with someone I hadn't seen in years, which wasn't the case.

Blake dropped out of college only a couple of months ago, after all.

Following him out of the fraternity, I opened the door of his car as we both sat down in it. He turned on the engine, drove out, and I couldn't stop looking at… his crotch. It was like something about it was calling out to me. And he looked more masculine now, driving the car with so much confidence.

I noticed him pulling up the corner of his lips, not thinking much of it. After all, even though I stared at his crotch for a little while longer than I should, I couldn't think that he suspected something was up.

Seconds later, he pulled over and we stepped out of the car. He took the lead and opened the door. His friend, the one that was holding the party, greeted us and we went to the kitchen, where everyone was dancing and filling their bellies with cheap drinks.

And then... I didn't know what was going to happen, but something was telling me it was going to be ground-breaking.

CHAPTER 2

Blake? Now, where was that guy? I asked myself, walking along the hallway as I started to hear thumps and huffs coming from one room. I didn't want to think much of it, so I just rushed over there without making much noise. Whoever was in the room and whatever they were doing, I shouldn't be worried about it. I was just going there to make sure that Blake wasn't there.

After all, the party was already ending and he needed to take me back home. I had a midterm tomorrow morning and I needed to go to bed right away.

I stopped in front of the door where the huffs and thumps were coming from, my ears finally noticing something I ignored before. They were having sex. No denying it. Those huffs, moans, and thumps – I knew what they meant.

And they made me feel insecure about myself. I had never had sex… Not even with my girlfriend. We were planning on doing it, but she was being hard about it. She kept saying that she was only going to do it with me when she was ready.

As for me, that wasn't only making me feel insecure about myself, but also a little annoyed with her. One of these days, I was going to have to be very honest with her and say just how much I wanted to change that.

I closed my hand and started to lift it, not understanding what was going on in my mind anymore. What the hell was I planning on doing? I asked myself. Was I really going to bust into the room and destroy the little fun they were having?

The question popped up in my mind, anger rising in my heart. I didn't know what was about it, but I was anything but my normal self right now.

I lowered my hand, wrapping it around the doorknob and then I twisted it. I thought it wasn't going to budge, but I was surprised when it did turn. I crept the door open and was happy when I noticed it didn't creak.

I inched my head into the room, noticing how dark it was. I couldn't see anything other than what the moonlight was revealing. And it was enough. I could see a man, huge, with a perfect body, pounding in and out of a woman's pussy. She was moaning so loudly that I almost had to cover my ears.

I only didn't do so thanks to it being part of my live sexual fantasy. And not only that, but it was also turning me on. It was much better than watching porn on my computer. I wanted to be right there in the action, and it was such a pity that I couldn't. The guy was ravaging her ass and was making me wonder if I could have the same performance if and when I did it with my girlfriend.

My hand went under my pants and I started to stroke my cock, doing so slowly. From where I was, I was mesmerized when I saw beads of sweat covering their bodies. I even noticed that the bed sheets were soaked with their sweat. I suddenly wished I could sniff them.

My dick was bigger in my hand and I even stopped remembering that I was still in the hallway of his friend's house. Anyone could find me doing this, even record me, and I wouldn't be able to do anything about it.

And the most curious thing about this? It was the fact that my eyes were more focused on the man than on the girl. I was telling myself that I was letting it happen this way because I wanted to take some notes on the way he was destroying her pussy, but anyone with keen eyes would notice that something else was going on with me.

My dick was so warm right now and I could feel that I was reaching my climax. What was I even thinking I was doing? I thought, rubbing my hand against my dick over and over, increasing my pace to what was beyond normal.

Not much longer from now and I'd be coming in my pants, which was something that happened often with me, but not in this manner. Not where I could be caught, and certainly not while I was spying on a couple having sex.

But I was so invested in what I was doing that it couldn't be stopped anymore. Seconds later, my dick was throbbing and a little moan escaped my mouth. Still creaming in my pants and feeling that release washing through my whole body, I couldn't help but feel a little bad about myself, even though it didn't last longer than a couple of seconds.

When it was over, I noticed that the guy was none other than Blake! I'd have spotted those earrings miles away, I thought, stepping away from the door as I took my hand out of my pants.

But just when I was doing that, Blake said, "Hmm? Who's there?" And I didn't know what to do. I scrambled away from the door, losing my balance and falling butt-first on the floor.

I didn't consider myself a big man, but the thump was all the evidence they needed. They now knew that someone was outside the room, and I was pretty sure they were going to come to investigate.

Coming to that conclusion, I jumped back up as I tried spinning around and getting out of there as soon as possible. But Blake was already throwing the door open and widening his eyes when he noticed that someone was in the hallway. He knew that someone was spying on him having hex, and he wanted to know the rest.

"Hey, you. Turn around and look at me. You think that doing what you were doing is okay?" He said, his voice rumbling across the hallway. Freezing, I couldn't help but obey him. My heart was tight. I didn't know what he was going to think once he saw my face, but it couldn't be anything good.

When he noticed it was me, he was looking at me as if he was disappointed.

"Tom? What the hell are you doing here?" He asked, stepping toward me as I noticed he didn't have his pants on. He did have his underwear on, but it wasn't enough.

My eyes kept going down, stealing glances at his impressive bulge. It was like it didn't even belong to him, and it was so big that my bulge didn't hold a candle to it. I could only imagine how big his cock was and what he made that girl feel.

I bet she was enjoying it. Part of me – even though I didn't want to think it was true – wanted me to replace her and be on the receiving end. He was pounding in and out of her so hard that I was pretty sure she was feeling like she couldn't walk anymore.

"It's nothing. It was nothing."

He folded his arms over his chest, making his muscles bulge. I couldn't help but wonder what I would feel if I were to put my hand on his biceps, pressing my fingers against them as I felt how strong his muscles were. I was pretty sure that such a thing would never happen, but the thought was still in my mind and I couldn't do anything to quench it.

"Sorry, man, but I don't believe you. I have nothing against you, but I think you're lying."

Not knowing what to say, I opened and closed my mouth over and over. I was looking like such a fool in front of him that I was pretty sure he was changing his opinion of me.

He took a step toward me, narrowing his eyes slightly. I knew what he was thinking. He knew that his suspicion was right. He knew that I'd been watching him having sex with that chick.

"I'm disappointed in you. I thought we were friends and that we trusted each other."

Still opening and closing my mouth over and over, I couldn't help but wince when he put his hand on my shoulder. I felt how warm and heavy it was, my body wishing that he was touching me with it, feeling every curve and part of me. I knew it would never happen, but my body couldn't stop thinking about those things, and that was annoying.

Nevertheless, my dropout friend had a distinct look in his eyes and I knew that meant something else was at play here.

I didn't know what it was, but my mind was so curious about it that, even before he said anything, I knew I was going to go along with it.

CHAPTER 3

Blake was a little out of himself that night. Nothing happened since then. We were together again, watching a movie. He was kicking back and drinking, watching the TV with a dirty smile on his face. I didn't know what that meant, but he was, once again, without a shirt and pants on.

I didn't know if he was teasing me, and I couldn't stop looking. I couldn't stop stealing glances at his massive bulge. He wore a dark pair of briefs that really highlighted his pearl white skin. I wanted to touch it even though I couldn't stop telling myself that I should never do it. Not to mention that my girlfriend could walk into the house and find us like this.

I even kept glancing out the window to see if she was going to show up soon or not. Feeling relieved that nothing of importance was happening outside, I tried to focus on the movie, even though that was a lost cause. Why was that guy killing the other? I didn't know and didn't care anymore at this point.

My heart was tight and I was feeling a little nervous. Blake had his legs open, knowing that his time in the fraternity house was coming to an end. It was his last night here, to be more precise. I didn't even want to think about it. I knew I was going to miss him a lot.

He put his drink down on the side table, glancing at me with a dirty smile still on his face.

"I still remember what happened that night, bro," he said, his voice a little altered, as if he was trying to convey that he knew something was up.

"I don't know what you're talking about," I said, feeling a little hard. I couldn't deny it. The way things were happening – and what was happening – was a real turn-on.

It was like Blake was right in front of me, pushing me against a wall and shooting me with several questions as he tried to find out everything about me.

And just like all the other times I'd been with him, I could smell his perfume. He always wore it. It was so strong that I couldn't smell anything else, which was saying something.

"But you do," he argued, pointing his finger at me. "You are a virgin, right? Don't lie to me. If you do, I'll be very disappointed and you know what I'm like when I am."

I didn't know what to say, opening my mouth and closing it, my eyes diverting down every so often as I tried not to let that side of me come out.

Dammit. He couldn't find out that I harbored feelings for him.

I looked down at my crotch, remembering that what he said was true. I was a virgin and I was so insecure about it. I mean, I was in college now, and pretty much everyone I knew had already lost their virginity.

"There's no need to feel ashamed of it. I thought you had a girlfriend. She never tried doing it with you?" He asked, his body glistening under the light coming from the screen.

I wasn't going to deny it. I wanted, one day, to wrap my lips around his nipples and feel what they were like against them. I wanted to do that and a lot more, even though I knew it was never going to happen.

"I'm trying, but she doesn't budge. She's just being careful about it and I don't know why. I know it's what I want, but I'm not in a hurry. It doesn't bother me."

He cackled, standing up on his couch and coming toward me. My heart started to speed up. It was one thing Blake sitting on a couch a couple of feet across from me and another to have him standing right in front of me. I couldn't even look at his face. My eyes kept going up and down, staring at his crotch, then his abs, and even at his perfect chest.

I wanted to feel his skin with my hands even though I knew it would never happen.

"That's not true. It bothers you quite a lot, doesn't it?" He asked, his hand going for his crotch before he gave it a little rub. My dick twitched in my pants. That was so hot and I couldn't even say that to him, which was infuriating.

Part of me wanted to tell him everything that was going on in my mind.

With just his underwear on, he took a step closer to me as he realized I wasn't even looking at his eyes.

"Bro, I know what's going on, and it's okay to look. Really. I was in a very similar situation before. I know what you're going through," he said, his voice lower all of a sudden. I didn't know why he was trying to be so sensual to me right now, but it was working and I was questioning if I really was straight.

I cleared my throat as I said, "I think you're mistaken about it. I'm not-"

"Gay?" He said, chuckling. "No point in lying to yourself or me. There's something about me you don't know, but I think you're going to like it when you do."

"What the hell are you talking about?" I asked when I realized that his shaft was growing thicker and harder in his underwear. Seeing that, I couldn't help but gulp.

He was so big. No wonder his last partner was huffing and moaning so loudly when they were having the time of their lives.

He got on his knees in front of me. For the first time now, I was looking at his eyes and I didn't know what to say. It was as though a lot of things were swirling in my mind and I had no hope of ever controlling them.

Blake moved his hand up, cupping my bulge. "Hmm, it's pretty big…"

I couldn't help but wonder if this was some kind of dream. But then, feeling his hand pressing against my bulge a little harder, I knew that such a thing couldn't be. This was indeed happening, and I didn't control it.

He licked his lips slowly.

"There's always something special with virgins, isn't there? It wasn't the first time I caught you looking, you know," he murmured, lowering his head toward my crotch, making me feel harder than I'd ever been. I couldn't help but notice the stain of pre-come on his underwear, showing me he was feeling just as turned on.

I didn't even know how to react to that, just that things were taking such a wild turn and I couldn't stop them. My breathing was quickening and I could feel the air around me getting hotter.

"You know that this is gay…" I said, my voice so feeble right now.

"And what of it? We've been friends for so long that I've been wondering about it this whole time."

"Wondering… what?" I asked, his hand massaging my balls and making me wonder what was going on in his mind. Could it be that, this whole time, he was bisexual? Blake couldn't be gay. After all, he ate the ass of that chick at that party. Was he hiding feelings from me he felt ashamed of?

And now that he finally had the moment he'd been waiting for all along, he was taking advantage of it.

It was dark outside, the moon rising above the buildings.

"Wondering how big you are," he replied, sneaking his fingers under my pants as he started to lower them. I had the opportunity to stop him, but I decided not to do it. The truth was that I wanted this to go on and I couldn't squander the chance.

He licked his lips again as I lifted my butt so that he could finish lowering my pants. His eyes were glinting with excitement when he finally saw my bulge.

The lust that he was feeling right now was almost palpable.

"Damn, bro. I knew you were big, but I didn't think you were so big."

Hearing that coming out of his mouth, I couldn't help but feel a little proud of myself.

"You haven't seen anything yet."

CHAPTER 4

Blake looked up, finding my eyes. "Obviously."

After a moment of silence, he added, "You have nothing to be ashamed of. Your girlfriend doesn't know what she's missing."

"Are you going to do what I'm thinking you are?" I asked, feeling a little happy that this was happening. I spent so much time trying to have sex with my girlfriend, only for my supposedly straight friend to be doing it with me now.

He was still massaging my bulge with his hand, his fingers applying the right amount of pressure when needed to. He was teasing me. I was so hard that my pre-come was seeping out.

"I just might. I need your confirmation first, though," he said and when I nodded, he started to lower my pair of briefs. He did so slowly, taking in what his eyes were seeing. He was so hungry that he was drooling from the sides of his mouth.

I couldn't believe that this was happening. I was going to have sex – or at least, something that resembled it – with my dropout friend and I was going to have to keep that behind several locked doors. My girlfriend could never find out.

"Perfect."

Just as he finished saying that, my dick came out, bouncing up and down as he kept on smiling like the devil he was. I didn't know if Blake was bi, but he was more than curious about me, that was for sure.

Pre-come still oozing out of the slit, he wrapped his fingers around my cock and gave it a little stroke, making me feel more pleasure than I ever thought possible. I moaned, tilting my head backward.

"How did that feel? Good?" He queried, now moving his hand up and down slowly, jacking me off. The way he was doing that, so slowly, was really turning me on and my body was getting hotter as the seconds ticked by.

"Bro, I don't even know what's happening anymore," I said as I closed my eyes and let the heat of the moment wrap me inside of it.

"You've been waiting for this for so long I feel like it's my duty to be doing it," he said as he ceased jacking me off before moving his hand down and cupping my balls again.

His hand was big enough to cup both of them, the way he was moving them between his fingers highlighting his experience. I felt afraid to ask it, but I wondered if that experience came from him jacking himself off or doing the same for other guys. I didn't think I'd ever know the answer.

"I feel so guilty right now."

He stopped what he was doing, looking up at me. When I re-opened my eyes, our eyes locked and I knew that our friendship, from now on, would never be the same.

"Why?" He asked, putting his fingers around my shaft again and stroking it up and down slowly, making me feel that I was going to come very soon. "Is it because of your shitty girlfriend? If it is, let me tell you this: she doesn't deserve you. You need someone better than her."

I had no idea what was happening anymore, what we were even talking about, but the way he was working my shaft with his hand was bringing me so much pleasure I couldn't hold back my moan when it jumped out.

He smiled, hearing that.

My come smeared his hand, making the friction almost nonexistent. My body was hotter than it had ever been, and I didn't know I'd been missing *so much* in my 19 years of existence. My girlfriend should have been more willing to do it with me. Thinking that, I couldn't help but wonder if dating her was even worth it anymore.

I decided not to think too much about that, focusing on this experience that I was having with my friend.

My eyes diverted down, finding his cock. Without even knowing what I was doing, I snuck my fingers under his pair of boxer briefs and ripped it off of him, finally freeing his massive dong. Blake said that I was big, but he was just being nice to me.

He was so much bigger than me I couldn't even put it into words and I didn't know how to cope with that. All I knew was that his dick was impressive and was pointing right at me. Blake was still on his knees, but I wanted to reach out and give him a blowjob, knowing that the thought would never have crossed my mind before.

"You really like what you're seeing. I've got to say – I never thought that this would happen one day. I always thought that you were as straight as an arrow."

I chuckled, noticing that he was just joking. And I couldn't do anything when he wrapped his lips around my cockhead, giving me so much pleasure I couldn't control it. The way he was applying pressure was unlike anything I'd experienced before.

And then, he started to move his head up and down along my cock, going all the way down to my pubes. I couldn't control him, bathing myself in the heat of the moment.

His other hand was working my balls, squeezing them slightly. He knew when and how to apply the right amount of pressure, working on all of my pressure points. My body was shaking and I knew that I was soon going to be coming inside his mouth, which was something I thought would never happen.

Our friendship would never be the same after this.

I put my hand on the back of his head, grabbing his hair as I started to dictate the pace I wanted. He was fine with that, moaning in acceptance.

The seconds ticked by, so much going on right now it was mind-blowing that I was still conscious. I thought I'd already have passed out and I was happy that I hadn't.

I felt my dick throbbing and I couldn't do anything to stop it when it was already happening. I worried that Blake was going to pull back right away, but he didn't. The dropout kept my dick trapped inside his mouth, swallowing every drop of my come.

Seconds later, he finally pulled back, some of my come on his lips. He locked his eyes with me, telling me a million things through them.

"It was so salty and I love it," he purred, his hand moving down and his fingers going around his dick. I couldn't help but lick my lips. I didn't lose my virginity per see, my head already going through all the possibilities of what was happening.

If he was so willing – and he pretty much was – then there was no point in denying the thing that was sprouting up in his mind. I never thought that this was something we would ever do together, but it was also true I'd said that so many times already there was no point repeating myself.

He took a step toward me and I lowered my head, feeling the powerful aroma of his perfume – and also the scent of his balls. I put my lips around his bulbous cockhead, not knowing what I should be doing right now. It was one thing thinking that I could give head and another putting it into practice.

This was unlike anything I did in my life, and I thought it was not just going to change our friendship, but also my life.

"Damn. I didn't think you were so hungry for it," he murmured, grabbing a handful of my hair and dictating the pace that he wanted from me. There was one thing that I could do to make him feel more pleasure than he ever did in his life before, and I was putting it into practice.

I licked and swirled with my tongue along the underside of

his dickhead, loving how it was already throbbing in my mouth. I thought it was going to take him a while until he was coming and climaxing, but it looked like I was wrong about that.

He was moaning, a certain thought popping up in my mind. It wasn't going to happen, right? I asked myself, realizing that after everything that happened, it just might.

Seconds later, he started to come into my mouth and it was the best feeling ever. His release was very creamy, sticky, and salty. I was loving all of it, which was something I thought I would never say.

Seconds later, he pulled out and fell on the couch by my side. Not saying anything, he was trying to catch his breath. We hadn't even penetrated each other, but the sex we had was already the best of our lives.

He locked his eyes with me and I knew he was thinking the same thing.

CHAPTER 5

My girlfriend was bawling her eyes out as she rushed out of the fraternity house, going to her car. She threw the door open, fell onto the seat, and turned on the engine of the small coupe. Then, she pulled out of the driveway and blasted toward the nearest intersection, where she took a left and then disappeared.

I didn't come clean with her about what happened between me and Blake, but there was no point in being her boyfriend anymore. I wasn't happy with her, which was something that took me a while to figure out.

I was happy with Blake, who was already showering. I closed the door slowly and then went over to the second floor, where I could see the steam coming through the gap of the door. I knew he had left it semi-open for me to go inside. He was waiting for me, and my dick was hard for him.

I wrapped my fingers around the doorknob as I pushed the door open, closing it slowly. He was in the shower cubicle, where I couldn't see his body. I could see the reflection of it through the glass, but it was distorted. Nevertheless, I could see his cock and balls, noticing the fact that he had shaved the night before.

He knew that this moment was going to come. He had already even bought everything we were going to need, including a bottle of lube. My hand was shaking, but I knew that I wanted to do this. To shower with another guy? If someone had said that to me before, when I was still with my girlfriend, I would have said that they were crazy.

Now, it felt like the right thing to be doing.

"Is it over?" Blake asked, referring to me and my girlfriend.

I nodded, not saying anything. It didn't matter how much time we spent together, I was always going to feel nervous around him.

So much so that he was the one that opened the door of the cubicle, finally showing me what he was like with no clothes on and when his body was covered with water.

Seeing the light reflecting off of his body, the water flowing around his perfect curves, I couldn't help but feel hard. I stepped inside the cubicle and closed the door, doing so more slowly than I would like. He was smiling, showing me his perfect teeth.

"Why are you so nervous? No need to feel that way about this. You know what I'm going to do with you when we are done," he said, taking off my clothes before I wetted myself. I was so nervous and not my normal self right now that I didn't even remember to take off my clothes after entering the bathroom.

"You were so clumsy, Tom," he said, kicking my clothes out of the cubicle after he reopened the door.

I couldn't help but smile, my dick so hard it was jutting out. As soon as he noticed that, he wrapped his fingers around it and started to pump it, doing so very slowly, as if to show me he was going to take his time.

"You're so nervous right now. Why are you feeling that way? I'm here to make you feel happy," he murmured into my ear, moving so that his body was pressing against mine, soaping me with his hands.

The soap and the water were removing any shreds of friction that there would otherwise be, and I couldn't help but wonder if that was what I was going to feel like when he was inside of me, taking my ass' virginity.

Still pressing our bodies against each other, we started moving around in the cubicle, just letting the water flow around our bodies. I could feel the warmth of his body pulsing to me, my hand going down and squeezing his ass cheek.

I thought he was going to feel a little impressed by what I did, but he wasn't. He was still looking at me with mischievous eyes, showing me that our shower was going to end only one way.

When he was tired of pumping my shaft, he put his hand on my shoulder and ordered, "Turn around. I think you want to do things a little faster this time."

"What do you mean?" I asked, his hands moving down and settling on my waist. Fully naked, I felt more exposed than ever before, knowing that this was going to end only one way.

"You will see," he murmured, moving so that his body was on top of me, covering me and making me feel so small I thought he was twice my size. I could feel his strong, warm chest against my back and his cock nudging my orifice.

He wasn't even going to use lube like I thought he was going to. He was going to penetrate me without it, and I knew it was going to be painful. Did I think he couldn't do it? Of course not. He was going to penetrate me with all of his might and it was going to be the most amazing thing in the world.

My body was already shivering.

He slid his hand over my shoulder, showing me he was going to be careful. I could tell that Blake had been in this situation many times before. He was going to make use of all his experience to make it unforgettable for me, and it was working. I could already tell that.

"You don't need to worry about it. You don't need to fear anything. You've always thought that you were straight, but that was nothing more than bullshit. You are as gay as I am."

I couldn't even try to say that he was wrong. He wasn't and he proved that to me with every passing second.

I couldn't wait until he was inside of me.

CHAPTER 6

ut then he patted me on my shoulder, moving away from me. Spinning around, I couldn't help but bulge my eyes as I wondered what was happening. He kept his dirty smile on his face, looking at me with mischievous eyes. I always thought I knew more or less what was going on in his mind, but this time, it was a mystery.

He turned off the showerhead, dried himself with a towel, and then walked out as I tried to follow him. I rubbed my body with the towel – the same one he used to dry himself – and then I scrambled after him, hitting my toe against the doorway.

By following his wet foot stains on the floor, I caught him in my bedroom, holding a butt plug in his hand. He was looking at me from behind it with devilish eyes, concocting a plan in his mind.

And when he spoke, it was like he had full control over me.

"Come toward me."

And I obeyed, going toward him until I couldn't anymore. He put his hand on my chest, moved it up to my shoulder, and then pressed it down until I was on my knees. When he was satisfied with it, he made me go on all fours and I did so with a big smile on my face.

Then, he made me part my legs, which I did with a huge smile on my face. He was going to insert the butt plug into my anus, stretching me out for his rough entry. Blake didn't want to hurt me too much, which was something that relieved me and disappointed me at the same time.

Fearing his disapproval, I said nothing. I felt the air going into my exposed orifice, loving the way he was treating me right now. It was like he was making me feel that my life had always been like this.

He lowered his head, murmuring something into my ear. When he pulled his head back, I couldn't help but feel jitters of excitement throughout my body. He said something about me becoming his bitch for the rest of my life, and I was excited about that. Doing what we were every day would make my life feel so complete I couldn't wait for it anymore.

He lubed up the butt plug and then my orifice, inserting it inside my rectum. I winced as I shut my eyes as tightly as possible, knowing that now I only needed to wait a couple of minutes until my orifice was wide enough for him.

He kissed the nape of my neck, his strong and naked body loving me the way he could. He murmured more phrases into my ear as he melted me for all the dirty plans he had in store for me. I just couldn't wait for a second longer as I felt impatient. I couldn't wait until this jock was pounding in and out of me, the same way he fucked that girl at that last party we went to.

Moments later, he pulled the buttplug out and I felt like I was missing something. He tossed it away, pushing his big, massive dong against my entrance. He nudged it and tried it for a couple of seconds, finally breaching through the last barrier when he felt he was ready.

The buttplug helped, but it didn't vaccinate me against the pain. It was flaring all over my body, making me shut my eyes again and wince strongly. Blake was so long that he was hitting my prostate and that was something I never thought I'd be thinking.

After all, I'd always thought that I was straight. Now, a gay guy would look at me and say that I could never have fooled him.

"How are you feeling right now?" He murmured, rolling his hips slowly and carefully. Just like I thought it was going to happen, Blake was being careful with me. I was still feeling a lot of pain all over my body, but it was okay. We were sharing such a strong, intimate moment that I didn't want it to end.

As Blake fucked me slowly, he moved his arm around my body and grabbed my iron. He started pumping it slowly, matching the rhythm of his hips. I started moving my body however I could, but I couldn't match him thrust for thrust.

"Better than ever," I breathed, loving how this was happening. Every time he pounded against my prostate, I felt ripples of pleasure swirling all over my body.

"Good. It's good to hear that," he said, picking up his pace moments later, ramming it in and out of me. My vision was darkening and I had no idea what was going to happen, just that I had never felt so much pleasure in my life. I wasn't a virgin anymore and that was something I wanted to tell everyone. Even though I was probably going to keep the fact that I wasn't straight anymore hidden, I would eventually tell everyone that I was now Blake's bitch.

Slapping sounds echoed in the room until he froze, his dick throbbing and shaking inside my rectum. What happened afterward changed me forever. He started to shoot out his milk, filling me with his release, and everything was bliss for me. His hand stopped pumping my dick when I also started to climax. I never thought that it was possible to reach our orgasm together, and I was so happy that it happened during our first time.

Blake stayed inside of me as he caught his breath, only pulling out when we both fell on my bed. He didn't wrap his arms around me, but I snuggled up on his chest and closed my eyes.

While I didn't know what the next days had in store for me, I knew they were going to mark my life forever.

The End

Looking for the first two books of the series? Find them below. The next page has a steamy sneak peek. Go check it out, too!

1. Caught Looking by the Quarterback
2. Caught Looking by the Basketeer

Lastly, leave a review if you liked the book. It always helps me so much!

SNEAK PEEK: CAUGHT LOOKING BY THE QUARTERBACK

Straight to Gay First Time Story (Bicurious Guys - 1)

I was just a college guy, like all the others. I was trying to fit in and look less like an idiot. Why did I have to stumble into the college's football team, though? I didn't know, but things were working out this way. More and more girls were beginning to show interest in me, even if it was only momentary… and I didn't think it was going to lead anywhere.

I sighed, closing the door by my side when I realized someone was there. Not too far from me, taking off his shirt and getting ready to put on his uniform. I supposed it was appreciation more than anything that was making me feel this way about the guy, even though I was 100% straight. Really, I was, and nothing was going to change that.

But nothing could have gotten me ready for what I was seeing. The guy was perfect. He was in his early twenties, so he was a little older than me, huge, with rippling muscles, and a beard still to be made. His hair was jet-black and his eyes the color of emerald. Every time he looked at me, he froze me with his gaze.

I couldn't stop thinking about him, even when he was in his room and wasn't doing anything more than playing on his computer. I wasn't going to say I was gay. I really wasn't, but I couldn't stop admiring him for being everything I wanted to become. Perhaps he could help me with working out at the gym, but then I didn't know if I'd be able to hide my boner... like it was happening now.

Not only I wasn't gay, but I also had to keep reminding myself that I wasn't a virgin, either. Not in the usual, more common sense of the word, at least. I had some experiences where it kind of happened with some girls... And I'd like to keep things at that.

Austin was now taking off his pants too, and I couldn't stop dissecting his perfect legs with my eyes. I couldn't help but imagine what it would be like to slide my hands over his muscles, feeling his hair, the curves that defined his legs, and smelling the scent of his crotch. Why was I thinking about those things of my team's leader?

I didn't know, but I was already feeling desperate and my boner was beginning to show. I came here with a common pair of jeans and it should be enough to keep it hidden. Austin could never find out that I had a huge turn-on for him, or else there would be trouble. This was a small college in the middle of nowhere, in a region known for being pretty homophobic. I didn't want to take the risk and then be forced to transfer to another university. It wasn't going to happen.

I took a deep breath and looked away quickly when he turned slightly. I didn't know if he was looking at me or not. We were in the dresser room and everything was pretty quiet here. Everything was so silent I could almost hear a pin dropping. I was a couple of feet away from Austin and I was pretty sure he wasn't thinking anything odd was happening here. After all, he had no reason to believe I was gay.

I took a deep breath in, looked back where he was, and I realized he was back to putting on his uniform. But he was still taking off his socks this time. He wasn't looking as imperious as before because he was seated now, his back turned to me.

But it wasn't that seeing him that way was making him look any less lust-inducing than he was. Even now, my body was frozen and I hadn't made much progress in terms of putting on my uniform. I needed to do that when my cock wasn't so hard. I should be punching myself that I was feeling those things for the guy that was always so willing to help everyone out, but it was just... impossible to control my feelings.

I heard the door opening and I knew that meant that things here were going to get more complicated. I could hear them talking out loud, cracking jokes, and laughing. It was the rest of the team. They were walking into the dressing room and were going to see that I was stealing glances at the quarterback...

BICURIOUS SERIES AND MORE

EXECUTIVE SUBMISSION

1.Hard in the Office 1: A Straight to Gay MM Story

2. Hard in the Office 2: No Pity for the Miserable Incel

3. Hard in the Office 3: An Incel's Tale of Degrading Humiliation

4. Hard in the Office 4: Bending the Incel Boss

5. Hard in the Office 5: Taming the Incel Spy

6. Hard in the Office 6: Lectured by the Boss

OBEY ME

1. Prep School Obedience 1: A Straight to Gay MM Story

2. Prep School Obedience 2: Phil is Punished

3. Prep School Obedience 3: Phil is Lectured

ABOUT THE AUTHOR

Michael Levi's biggest passion? Writing steamy, romantic stories that leave his readers panting. He's currently focusing on Omegaverse steamy romances, but his collection is diverse and there are books for everyone's tastes. If you're looking for straight to gay, first time, BBC, ABDL, and more, you're going to find them on his author page.

He lives to pamper his readers, every kiss means a lot more than what meets the eye, and he loves his Alpha males. Making sure that every gay first time feels different, Michael Levi writes his stories with a cup of coffee by his side. And for inspiration, he always opens a photo of his new crush.